THE NOTEBOOK OF DOOM

FLURRY OF THE SNOMBIES

by Troy Cummings

BRANCHES

SCHOLASTIC INC.

TABLE OF CONTENTS

To Brooke: Hi, niece! Thanks for the Super-Squirrel
drawing. I still have it, hanging in my studio.

Camp Rule #417: Katie Carella and Liz Herzog are the best.
They should get merit badges for their terrific work.

No part of this publication may be reproduced, stored in a retrieval system, or transmitted in any form or by any means, electronic, mechanical, photocopying, recording, or otherwise, without written permission of the publisher. For information regarding permission, write to Scholastic Inc., Attention: Permissions Department, 557 Broadway, New York, NY 10012.

Library of Congress Cataloging-in-Publication Data

Cummings, Troy, author.
Flurry of the snombies / by Troy Cummings.
pages cm. — (The Notebook of Doom ; 7)
Summary: It is a very hot summer in Stermont, and Alexander and his friends are at Camp Gloamy in the mountains, but even here there are monsters—specifically zombie snowmen called snombies who want to freeze the young monster-hunters.
ISBN 0-545-79550-8 (pbk.) — ISBN 0-545-79551-6 (hardcover) — ISBN 0-545-79552-4 (ebook) — ISBN 0-545-79553-2 (eba ebook)
1. Monsters—Juvenile fiction. 2. Snowmen—Juvenile fiction. 3. Camps—Juvenile fiction. 4. Friendship—Juvenile fiction. 5. Horror tales. [1. Monsters—Fiction. 2. Snowmen—Fiction. 3. Camps—Fiction. 4. Friendship—Fiction. 5. Horror stories.] I. Title. II. Series: Cummings, Troy. Notebook of doom ; 7.
PZ7.C91494Fl 2015
813.6—dc23
[Fic]
2014035312

ISBN 978-0-545-79551-7 (hardcover)/ISBN 978-0-545-79550-0 (paperback)

10 9 8 7 6 5 4 3 2   19 20 21 22 23/0

Printed in China   62
First Scholastic printing, April 2015

Book design by Liz Herzog

1 FIRST DAY OF BUMMER

Alexander stepped out of his air-conditioned house and into a volcano. Actually, it wasn't a volcano. It was his front porch.

"Shake a leg, kiddo!" his dad shouted from the driveway.

"*Ugghhh,*" Alexander groaned. "It's a million degrees outside."

"You're right!" his dad said. "The perfect day to start summer camp!"

By the time Alexander got to the car, he was drenched with sweat.

"A week at Camp Gloamy will be super-neat!" his dad said. He tossed Alexander's sleeping bag into the trunk. "You'll learn great survival skills!"

Alexander slumped into the back seat. He already *had* great survival skills. Ever since moving to Stermont, he had survived being stomped, chomped, and swallowed by all kinds of monsters. He and his two best friends were members of a monster-fighting club called the Super Secret Monster Patrol. (S.S.M.P. for short.)

Alexander buckled his seat belt. "It's just . . ." he said. "I'm not really much of a camper."

"Oh, Al," his dad said, turning on the car. "Just give it a shot! I *loved* summer camp when I was a kid!"

Alexander sighed.

"And don't forget," his dad said. "Rip and Nikki will be there, too!"

Alexander smiled a little.

This week is going to be hot, stinky, and totally crummy, he thought. *But at least my best friends and I can be hot, stinky, and crummy together.*

2 UPHILL DRIVE

The car began winding its way up into the Gloamy Mountains.

The town of Stermont was laid out below like a bunch of dollhouses. Alexander could see the water tower, his crumbling old school, and the brand-new school where he'd be going this fall.

CR-RR-RRUNCH! Alexander's dad turned onto a gravel road. Alexander had spent plenty of time in the woods behind his house. But these woods felt *wilder*. The trees were taller, the hills were steeper, and the shadows seemed darker.

VWOOSH! Just up the road, something gray and fuzzy darted through the trees.

"Holy molars!" Alexander's dad shouted. "Did you see that?!"

Alexander gasped.

He grabbed a book from his backpack—the official S.S.M.P. monster notebook. Alexander never left home without it. He flipped it open.

SKEETER-COPTER

Two-headed mosquito
with spinning blades.

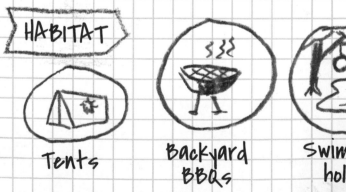

HABITAT

Tents

Backyard
BBQs

Swimming
holes

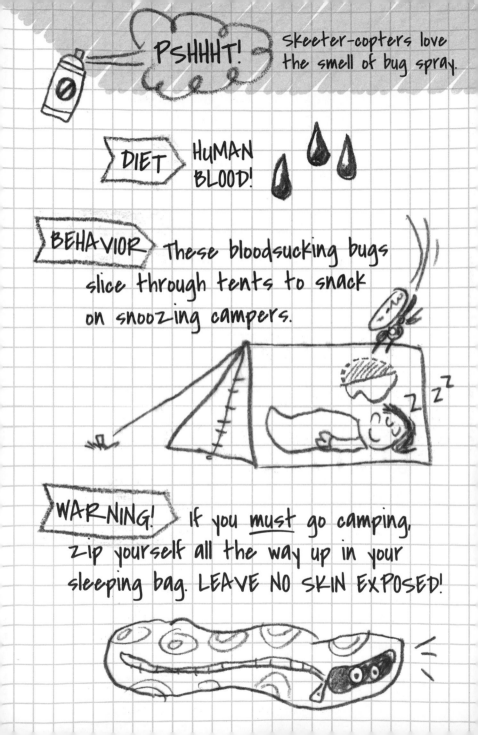

PSHHHT! Skeeter-copters love the smell of bug spray.

DIET HUMAN BLOOD!

BEHAVIOR These bloodsucking bugs slice through tents to snack on snoozing campers.

WARNING! If you <u>must</u> go camping, zip yourself all the way up in your sleeping bag. LEAVE NO SKIN EXPOSED!

"That vulture was huge!" said Alexander's dad.

Alexander snapped the notebook shut. *A plain old bird?* he thought. *That's not even close to a monster!*

They drove deeper into the forest. The gravel road became a dirt road. Then the dirt road became a narrow, weed-covered lane.

They came to a stop at a crooked gate.

CAMP GLOAMY

Alexander's dad turned off the car. "Well, here we are," he said.

They stepped out and looked around. The forest was silent.

"Where *is* everybody?" said Alexander.

CREAK! URGH! WHOOSH! A hairy beast-man leaped over the gate, landed with a grunt, and rushed toward Alexander.

3 STRANGE RANGER

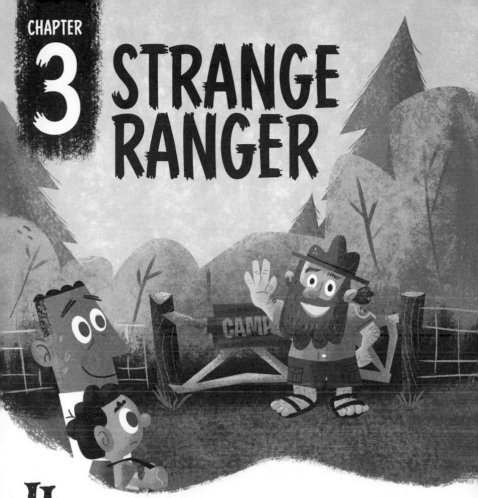

Howdy! I'm Ranger Harry!" said the man at the gate. He looked like a cross between a bear and a lumberjack. In sandals.

"Oh, hi!" said Alexander's dad. "Glad to see a friendly face!"

Ranger Harry knelt down by Alexander. He had a bushy ponytail, a shaggy beard, and the hairiest arms Alexander had ever seen. "You must be Alexander Bopp," he said. "You're the last chipmunk to arrive."

"Uh, yeah," said Alexander. He couldn't stop staring at the ranger's hairy feet. Even his *toes* were shaggy.

Ranger Harry opened the gate. "Say bye to your dad and go on ahead to the campfire circle!" he said.

Alexander grabbed his things from the car.

"Happy camping, Al!" said his dad, giving him a tight squeeze.

"See you in a week, Dad," said Alexander. He headed into the woods, and stopped when the path forked in different directions.

ARCHERY RANGE

CABINS

ROPE BRIDGE

LAKE GLOAMY

SALT MINES
CLOSED! KEEP OUT!

Great, thought Alexander. *There's no sign for* campfire circle. *I've been at camp for two minutes, and I'm already lost.*

"Salamander!" shouted a voice.

"Where have you been, Salamander?" shouted another voice.

Alexander grinned. Only two people called him Salamander: the other two members of the S.S.M.P.

"Rip! Nikki!" he shouted. He turned to see his friends running down the trail.

They were both soaked with sweat. Instead of her usual hoodie, Nikki wore a floppy yellow sunhat.

"What a hat!" said Alexander.

"Hat?!" said Rip. "It looks like a glob of pizza dough landed on her head!"

Nikki rolled her eyes. "This big hat keeps me shaded," she said. "It works better than sunblock."

Nikki was secretly a monster called a jampire. A *good* monster.

Alexander wiped the sweat from his brow. "So, guys," he said. "Which way should we go?"

"Beats me!" said Rip. "Ranger Scary sent us out on our own, too."

They tried a few trails, and finally found the campfire circle. Three other kids stood near an empty fire pit. Behind the pit was a hill of white grainy stuff that looked like sand. Ranger Harry stood on the hill.

"Hello, possums!" he shouted. "Welcome to Camp Gloamy!" He tugged at his beard. "*Hmm* . . . I thought there'd be more of you," he said. "Oh, well. Tell us who you are and why you're here."

"Get ready for the happiest, campiest week of your lives!" said Ranger Harry. "But also, get ready to learn how to survive!" He slid down the hill, raising a cloud of white dust. "The sun's about to set, so let's go to our cabins. Any questions?"

Alexander raised his hand. "Where did that big pile of sand come from?"

Ranger Harry laughed. "This isn't sand!" he said. "It's salt! Camp Gloamy was built on an old salt mine. Miners would dig up salt from inside this mountain. Then they'd ship it to restaurants, road crews, and pretzel factories."

Rip wiped his forehead on his sleeve. "Are you sure that salt didn't come from dried-up camper sweat?"

Alexander gave his own shirt a sniff. "*Ugh.* Our week at camp is really going to stink."

CABIN FEVER

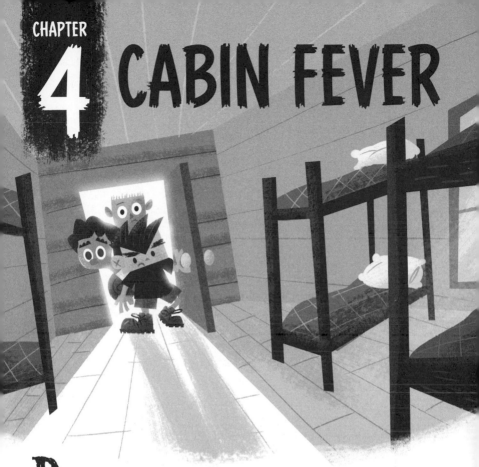

Dibs on the top bunk!" said Rip, shoving his way into the boys' cabin.

"Okay, whatever," said Alexander. "There are plenty of beds. We can *all* have top bunks." He turned to their third roommate. "Leo, do you want the bed by the window?

"No, thanks," said Leo. He pulled out a night-light. "I'll take a spot where I can plug this in."

The boys played a few games of checkers before flopping into bed. The air was heavy, and a dim moonbeam peeked through the window.

"*Ugh,*" said Rip. "It's *sooo* hot. I'm baking like a potato."

"I'll open the window more," said Alexander.

"No!" cried Leo. He jerked his blanket over his face.

"*Ooooh,*" said Rip. "Maybe it's time for a ghost story!"

CLINK!

Alexander and Rip looked to the window.

"Did you hear something?" asked Leo.

CLINK-CLINK!

Alexander sat up. "It's coming from outside," he whispered.

"Yipes!" Leo burrowed further under his covers.

Rip stuck his head out the window.

"There's nothing there, guys," he said. "Just trees and mountains and junk like that."

"I bet it was a raccoon," said Alexander.

"That was no raccoon," Leo muttered from his blanket. "It was a ghost!"

"Oh, come on!" said Rip. "Ghosts aren't real!"

"Now, *monsters*, on the other hand . . ." added Alexander.

"Gaaaah!" Leo screamed.

"Oh, sorry," said Alexander. "Don't be scared. We're totally safe in our cabin."

Something pounded at the door! The boys shrieked.

CREEEEEEAK!

Ranger Harry stuck his bushy head in the cabin. "Nighty-night, badgers!" he said. "Camp Rule #44: Get a good night's sleep!"

SLAM!

The door closed. But the boys' eyes stayed open long into the night.

RISE AND WHINE

B LAARP-BLARBLE-BLAAARP!

Alexander woke to a buzzy, honking sound coming from outside.

"What *is* that?" he asked.

"A bird, maybe?" said Leo.

Rip yawned. "Or a barfing buffalo."

Or a super-loud monster! thought Alexander. He threw on some clothes. Then he peeked in the notebook while Rip and Leo were getting dressed.

BLUE-THORNED HONKFLOWER

Beautiful plant, ugly sound.

HABITAT Hiking trails.

DOODLE-DEE-DEE!

Honkflowers love clarinet music.

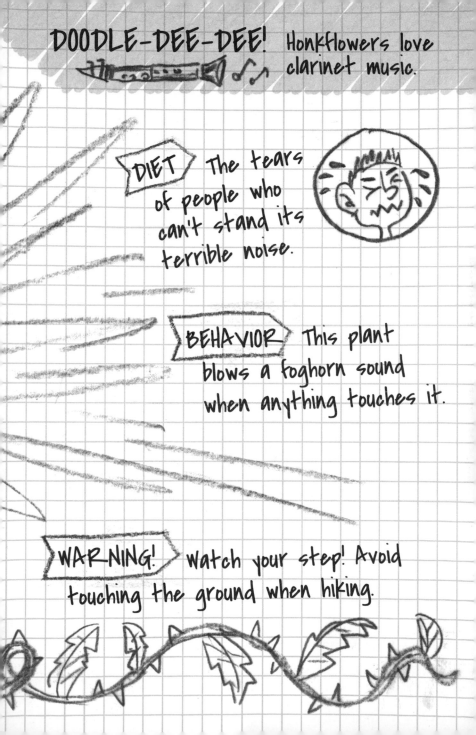

DIET The tears of people who can't stand its terrible noise.

BEHAVIOR This plant blows a foghorn sound when anything touches it.

WARNING! Watch your step! Avoid touching the ground when hiking.

"Let's go see what's making that noise," said Alexander, snapping the notebook shut. The boys stepped out into the hot morning air.

Nikki, Anna, and Dottie stood outside the girls' cabin, covering their ears.

BLAARP-BLARBLE-BLAAARP!

Ranger Harry marched along, blowing hard into a bugle. His cheeks were almost as red as his beard.

"Rise and shine, critters," he said. "It's chow time."

The ranger led the campers to a picnic table.

"For breakfast," he said, "we're having piping-hot salt mush. And to wash it down, a steamy mug of onion cider."

Alexander sniffed a spoonful of salt mush.

Rip pushed his bowl aside. "Yo! Papa Bear!" he said. "This porridge is way too hot for this weather!"

Ranger Harry's eyes narrowed. "Camp Rule #81: Always eat a hot breakfast."

Rip sighed.

Alexander turned to Nikki. Her face was hidden by the brim of her floppy hat. "So," he said, "how was your first night in the girls' cabin?"

Nikki looked up. Her eyes were half-closed. "Lousy," she said. "I didn't get much sleep. I kept hearing this weird sound—"

"A clinking noise?" said Alexander.

"Yes!" said Nikki. "Like someone ringing a glass bell."

"Maybe it was a bunny!" said Dottie.

"Bunnies can't ring bells," said Anna.

DINK! DINK!

Ranger Harry tapped his spoon against his canteen. "Listen up, muskrats. Each of you will learn one survival skill this week."

He put a clipboard on the table.

ARCHERY — Anna
CANOEING — Nikki
TRAP-MAKING — Dottie
FIRE SAFETY — Rip
COOKING — Leo
MAPMAKING — Alexander

"Canoeing?!" said Nikki. "Awesome."

"Mapmaking?" said Alexander. "I wish I had gotten archery!"

"Mapmaking's better than fire safety!" said Rip. "Anything with *safety* in the name must be boring."

The campers lined up in the blistering sun to await orders from Ranger Harry. One by one, he gave them a tool and a set of instructions.

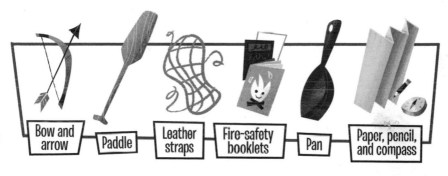

Bow and arrow / Paddle / Leather straps / Fire-safety booklets / Pan / Paper, pencil, and compass

"Nikki," he said. "Take this paddle and meet me at Lake Gloomy."

"Yes, sir!" said Nikki, smiling.

"Rip," he said. "Take these safety booklets and start reading!"

Rip groaned.

Ranger Harry made his way down the line to Alexander. "Take this paper, pencil, and compass. Your job is to map out our campgrounds," he said.

"Uh, okay," said Alexander.

Ranger Harry lifted his bugle.

BLAAAAAAAAARP!

"Now go!" he shouted. "Meet back here for lunch."

The campers scattered.

Alexander hiked all over camp, drawing his map. He saw a lookout tower, a rope bridge, and a few more mounds of salt.

Not bad, thought Alexander, folding up the map. *I hit every spot in camp.*

CLINK-CLINK!

Alexander jumped. *The noise from last night!*

The clinks sounded like ice cubes hitting a glass. They were coming from deep in the woods.

"Hello?" he called out. "Is someone there?"

Something hit him on the back of his head. Something wet. And cold!

PLOP! The icy thing fell from his head and splatted on the ground.

A snowball?! Alexander thought. *In* this *heat?!*

He looked around. Nobody was there.

Hmmmm . . . Alexander scooped up the lump of snow from the dry, cracked dirt. Then he remembered his first day in Stermont, when Rip had beaned him with a dodge ball.

"Good one, Rip!" he shouted, wiping the back of his neck. "Wherever you are!"

6 HOT LUNCH

A lexander tried to carry the snowball to lunch, but it melted on the way.

"Ah, the last porcupine!" said Ranger Harry, waving to Alexander. "You're just in time to learn Camp Rule #218: Lunch tastes better in the shade!"

Alexander plopped down in a shady spot near Rip and Nikki.

Ranger Harry held up a menu he'd carved from a chunk of wood.

LUNCH
Huckleberry sandwich (with mayo.)
Trail mix (Extra-chunky!)
Bug juice (Less chunky.)

"Eat up!" said Ranger Harry.

"Bug juice?" said Rip. *"Blecchh!"*

Nikki drank hers in one gulp. She gave Rip a big, red smile.

"You goofball," she said. "*Bug juice* is camp talk for fruit punch!"

CRUNCH! Alexander ate a handful of trail mix. It tasted like mixed-up bits of trail.

"Guess what?" he said. "I heard that strange clinking sound again! Just before I got smacked with Rip's slushball." He turned to Rip. "Where'd you find the snow, anyway?"

"Snow?!" said Rip. "How could there be snow here at Camp Sweatbox?"

Alexander nibbled on his sandwich. "Well, *somebody* splatted me."

"It wasn't me," said Rip. "I've been parked on that salt mound all morning reading about fire safety."

"And I've been canoeing!" said Nikki. "I can almost steer!"

Rip snatched the map from Alexander's backpack. "Okay, weenie. Let's see what *you've* been working on."

"Wow!" said Nikki. "Great map, Salamander!"

"Thanks," said Alexander. "But mapmaking's still not as fun as canoeing or archery or—"

"Or trap-making!" said Dottie. She held up a huge net woven from little straps. "I made it to catch pet bunnies!"

"That trap could catch fifty bunnies!" said Anna.

"Or a bear!" said Leo.

BLAAAARP! Ranger Harry blew into his bugle.

"Ranger Blare-y really needs a new horn," said Rip, plugging his ears.

"Listen up, squirrels," he said. "My beard is drooping. That means it's way too hot. So this afternoon we're going to rest in our cabins. Then tonight we'll take a long hike."

"Like, in the dark?" said Leo. He gulped. The campers trudged back to the cabins.

"Guys," Alexander whispered to his friends, "keep your, uh, ears peeled for that clinking sound. It could be coming from a monster!"

"A monster? Up here?" asked Nikki.

"I think this heat is really starting to get to you, Salamander!" said Rip.

"Maybe so," said Alexander, touching the back of his neck. *But where did that snowball come from? And how come my neck still feels cold?*

THE NIGHT HIKE

$\mathbf{T}$he hot, sweaty campers spent the afternoon resting in their hot, sweaty bunks. Finally, the sun set.

"It feels hotter now than it was at noon," said Alexander.

"If I sweat any more, I'll have to change my socks," said Leo.

Rip shook his fist at the moon.

"Come on, nature!" he shouted. "Cool off already!"

KNOCK-KNOCK!

Ranger Harry stuck his nose in the cabin. "Move it, woodchucks! It's time for our hike under the stars!"

Alexander, Rip, and Leo joined the girls outside. They all followed Ranger Harry up a trail surrounded by pine trees. They made their way up the mountain toward a small, calm lake.

"Nikki," whispered Alexander. "Rip and I didn't hear any clinking sounds this afternoon. Did you?"

"Nope," said Nikki. "Quiet as—Oh!" she pointed to a rack of canoes. "There's my canoe!"

"Okay, otters," said Ranger Harry. "Here we are! Beautiful Lake Gloomy."

The lake was like a mirror.
It reflected the moon, the trees,
and the sweaty faces of six
campers, ready to jump in.

"So," said Anna. "Can we go swimming?"

"You bet," said Ranger Harry. "Swimming is on tomorrow's schedule!" He blinked a few times. "Well, pluck my beard! We should have worn our swimsuits. We could have gone swimming tonight!"

The campers' shoulders slumped.

41

Ranger Harry fanned himself with his hat. "Um, how about this?" he said. "Why don't we test our mapmaker?"

Alexander's eyebrows shot up. "Huh?!"

"We'll race back to camp—boys against girls," said Ranger Harry. "Girls, you take the trail we just hiked. And Alexander, use your map to find a shortcut. I'll meet you all at the cabins."

"Super-lame!" said Nikki. "Why does it have to be boys versus girls?"

"Camp Rule #114: Listen to your ranger. He's smart as a moose!" said Ranger Harry. "Ready . . . set . . . scamper!"

"He's clearly making these rules up as he goes," mumbled Nikki. She jogged after the other girls.

"Last one there is a rotten pinecone!" shouted Rip.

Ranger Harry saluted the boys, and then headed down another trail.

"Ohmygosh," said Leo. "We're alone! At night! In the middle of the woods!"

"We're not alone," said Alexander. "We've got each other. Nothing will—"

CLINK!

"Uh-oh," said Leo, his voice shaking.

"There's that weird noise again," whispered Rip.

CLINK!

"It sounds like marbles in a jar," said Alexander.

CLINK!

"And it's getting closer!" said Leo.

8 COLD SHOULDER

Run!" yelled Alexander.

"Which way?!" cried Leo.

Alexander shook open his map. "Uh, this creek leads right behind our cabin. Come on!"

SPLISH! SPLOSH! The boys raced through the shallow creek.

CLINK!

"Where is that sound coming from?" shouted Rip. "Are we running away from it, or toward it?"

They stopped and looked around. The creek sparkled in the moonlight.

A branch shook.

Rip pointed to a cluster of shrubby trees. "Somebody's there," he whispered.

A figure in the shadows moved toward them. Its long, skinny arms poked out from the leaves.

"The ghost!" said Leo.

SPLISH! Leo fainted, landing in the creek.

But the figure lurching toward them wasn't a ghost. It was a snowman. A *moving* snowman. It rolled toward the boys, its head lolling to one side.

45

Rip and Alexander dragged Leo onto dry land.

"How is this possible?!" yelled Rip, taking a step back. "It's five thousand degrees! That snowman should be *melting*!"

"I told you I saw snow!" said Alexander.

The snowman came to a stop on the opposite side of the creek.

"Maybe it can't cross water," said Rip. He stuck his thumb on his nose and wiggled his fingers at the snowman. "You can't get us, slushbucket!"

The snowman glared at them so hard, one of its eyes fell out. Then the monster reached down and scooped a snowball out of its belly.

"No way!" said Rip.

The snowman whipped the snowball at Rip.
SPLOP! It smacked him in the face.

"Hey!"

PLAP! A second snowball hit Rip in the knee.

Alexander gasped. "This thing should be a major-league pitcher! Let's—"

PLOOF! A curveball hit Alexander's shoulder, knocking him to the ground.

"Salamander!" Rip shouted. "Are you okay?"

Alexander sat up. "I think so. But yow! That snowball was extra cold. My shoulder feels all numb."

"I know!" yelled Rip. "My knee is blue!"

The snowman looked down at its belly and frowned. Its middle ball now looked like an apple core.

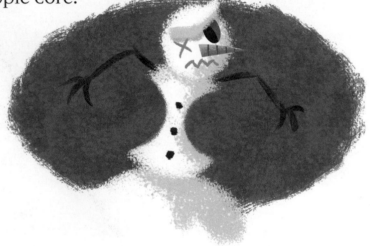

"It out-scooped itself!" said Alexander.

"Ha!" Rip shouted. "Looks like Frosty is low on snow!"

Then the snowman raised its stick arms and—**FLOOP!**—pulled off its head!

9 HEADS UP!

The snow monster tossed up its head and—**BAP!**—spiked it like a volleyball, straight for Rip.

The flying head stared at Rip with its one eye as it cannonballed through the night air.

"Duck!" shouted Alexander, tackling Rip.

The flying head missed Rip. But not Leo.

Leo blinked, and sat up. "Where's the ghost?! Why's my face cold?! Where'd this carrot come from?!"

Alexander and Rip looked back. The headless snowman had melted into a pile of slush.

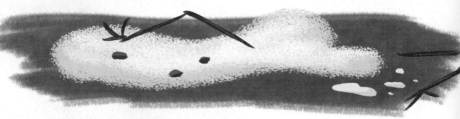

"*Hellooooo?*" called a voice. "It's almost lights-out! Back to your cabins, hedgehogs!"

Leo stood up. "That's Ranger Harry!"

"Yeah," said Alexander. "Our cabin is just over that hill, Leo. Why don't you run ahead? Rip and I will catch up."

"Cabins," said Leo. "Nice, safe cabins." He staggered up the hill.

Rip brushed the slush off his shorts. "So I guess that dumb old snowman couldn't get around without its head, huh?"

"It wasn't a snowman," said Alexander. He brought out the notebook and flipped through a few pages.

"It's in here somewhere," he said. "Let's see . . . pool-shark, frog-gobbler . . . snombie!"

SNOMBIE

Snowman + Zombie.

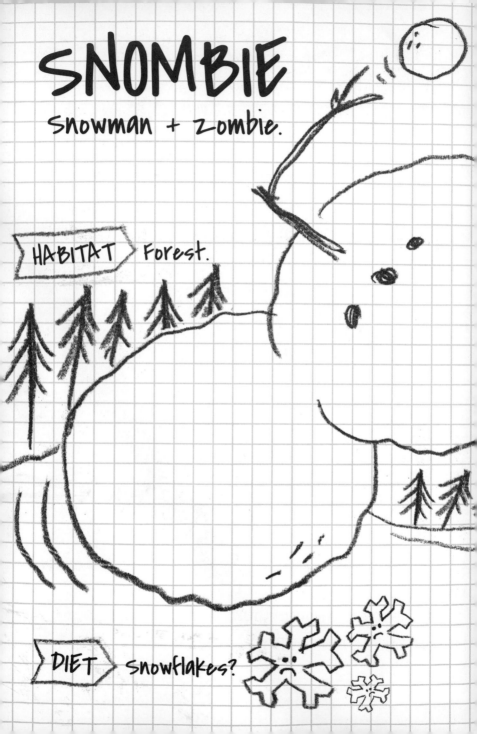

HABITAT Forest.

DIET Snowflakes?

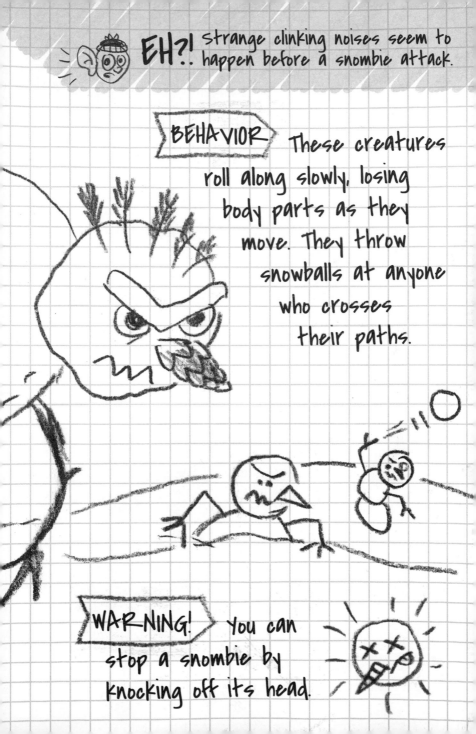

"Lucky for us, snombies are slow, dumb, and ugly!" said Rip. "We can handle an army of 'em."

"I hope we don't have to," said Alexander. "I'm exhausted from dodging *one* snombie. Let's get back. We'll fill Nikki in at breakfast tomorrow."

Suddenly, there were hundreds of clinks, close together, like someone angrily drumming their fingers on glass.

Alexander looked at Rip. They both ran to their cabin.

The clinks continued into the night.

10 SNOW DAY

Alexander heard a new sound when he awoke. The sound of his teeth chattering.

The cabin was *freezing!*

"Rip? Leo?" he said, sitting up. "Did you—" He looked around. Rip and Leo were gone.

"AAARGHH!!" Someone was shouting outside. Alexander tried to look out a window, but it was frosted over.

He hopped out of bed. He hadn't packed any warm clothes, so he threw on some shorts and a shirt over his pj's.

Then he opened the cabin door, and gasped. The entire camp was covered in a deep layer of snow. The other campers were running every-which-way, laughing and throwing snowballs.

Nikki and Rip tromped over, waving. Nikki had tied her yellow floppy hat down over her ears.

"Salamander!" said Rip. "While you were hibernating, I told Nikki all about the snombies."

"It's crazy," said Nikki. "Did *they* make this super-fun blizzard?"

"I don't know," said Alexander. "The notebook says they're made *from* snow, but it doesn't say anything about snombies *making* snow."

BLAAAAAAAAARP!

Ranger Harry marched out, still wearing shorts and sandals.

"This snow is terrific!" he said. "Now we can learn *winter* survival skills."

The ranger handed everyone a shovel.

Rip groaned.

"Camp Rule #19: Work to stay warm!" said Ranger Harry. "You'll all clear different paths around camp."

He brought out his clipboard.

SHOVEL DUTY
Alexander and Rip: Cabins
Nikki: Rope-bridge trail
Anna and Leo: Campfire circle

SALT DUTY
Dottie

Dottie raised her hand. "What's salt duty?" she asked.

"You'll be spreading salt on the snow to help it melt," Ranger Harry explained.

"Just like my dad salts our driveway in the winter!" Alexander said.

"Yup! And when everyone's finished," Ranger Harry said, "head to the campfire circle. We're going to cook s'lesses!"

"What are s'lesses?" asked Anna.

"They're like s'mores—" said Ranger Harry.

"Yay!" cheered the campers.

"But without the chocolate and the graham crackers," Ranger Harry continued. "And instead of marshmallows, I use dandelion patties."

"Booooo!" said the campers.

"Get busy, gophers," said Ranger Harry. "I'm going to find firewood." He headed to the trees.

Everyone began clearing their trails.

"Watch where you shovel!" said Dottie. "My bunny trap is *somewhere* under this snow."

Alexander and Rip dug a circle around the cabins. Nikki plowed her way over a hill.

After a few minutes, Alexander stopped shoveling. "Rip," he whispered. "Did you hear something?"

CLINK-CLINK!

"It's coming from over by the rope bridge!" Rip said.

"Nikki!" said Alexander.

They threw down their shovels and followed Nikki's footprints.

A round, snowy figure stood on the bridge.

"Is that the snombie from last night?" said Rip, squinting.

"It doesn't look the same . . ." said Alexander.

This one had no arms and no face. And it was wearing a floppy yellow sunhat.

11 SURPRISE INSIDE

The boys crouched behind a stump near the rickety old bridge.

"Why doesn't that snombie have a face?" Alexander whispered.

"Who cares?!" said Rip. "It stole Nikki's hat!" He stood up.

"Rip, no!" whispered Alexander. He grabbed Rip's elbow.

Rip broke free and charged onto the bridge, swinging his fists. "*Nobody* steals from the S.S.M.P.!" he shouted.

The snowman didn't move.

PLOFF! Rip knocked its head off with a single punch. He caught Nikki's hat before it hit the ground.

The snowman's body shook. Clumps of snow fell away from its middle ball, revealing a blue-faced girl with fangs and braces.

"Nikki!!!" Alexander ran over. He and Rip brushed away the snow.

"How did you get covered in snow?" Rip asked.

"The sn-sn-snombies g-g-got me!" she said, shivering. "I heard that clinking noise, and a bunch of snombies rose up from the snow! They clobbered me with snowballs until I was c-c-c-overed! I couldn't move! I think they were trying to FR-FR-FREEZE me!"

CLINK-CLINK!

"W-w-w-watch out! There's that n-n-n-noise again!" yelled Nikki.

RRRUUUUUGHHHRHRRR!!!

Four growling snombies rose up from the snow on the far side of the bridge. Some had broken sticks for arms. Some had lopsided heads. They all looked angry.

The bridge shook as the monsters rolled toward Alexander, Rip, and Nikki.

"Let's knock their blocks off!" said Rip.

"No way—there are too many of them!" yelled Alexander. "And besides, Nikki is still half-frozen!"

ZING! ZING! The snombies whipped dozens of snowballs through the air. The three friends ducked. Then they raced off the bridge.

"It's hard . . ." said Nikki, ". . . to run . . . in snow."

"Head to the salted path," said Alexander. "There's hardly any snow there!"

"Yeah," said Nikki. "And the snombies seemed to be avoiding that trail."

They soon made it back to the cabins, leaving the monsters behind.

"Luckily, snombies move slower than cold snot!" said Rip.

Nikki dashed into the girls' cabin. She came back out a minute later in dry clothes, wrapped in a towel.

"I'm warmed up, and ready for battle!" she said. "Let's—"

ARRGH!!

"Those screams are coming from the campfire circle!" said Rip.

"The other campers!" said Alexander. "We have to help them!"

CHAPTER 12 SNOWBALL FIGHT!

Alexander, Rip, and Nikki rushed to the campfire circle. Dozens of snombies had risen from the ground! They were pelting the other campers with snowballs.

"Hello, beavers!" said Ranger Harry, throwing a log on the fire. "You're just in time for a snowball fight! And look how many snowmen the other campers built! What fun!"

The campers were screaming and running around. But not because they were having fun.

"Why can't Ranger Harry see the monsters?" whispered Nikki.

"Who knows?" said Alexander, dodging a snowball.

"Camp Rule #594: Have a ball!" said Ranger Harry. "You three should join in while I go get more firewood."

He dragged his sled toward the woods.

"Fire . . . that's it!" said Rip. He scrambled up the salt mound to get a better look. "There are no snombies near the campfire. They're staying back!" He slid down.

CLINK-CLINK-CLINK-CLINK!

More snombies rose up.

"See that?" said Alexander. "New snombies pop up every time there's a clink."

"You're right!" said Rip, sidestepping a couple more snowballs. "And whatever's doing the clinking is up by the lake. That's where the sound seems to be coming from."

Leo stumbled over, half covered in snow. "Ohmygosh!" he screamed. "We're knocking these snowmen apart, but they keep rising back up! It's like they're zom-zom-zombies!"

Alexander grabbed Leo's shoulders. "Leo, listen to me. Tell Dottie and Anna to stay near the campfire. These, uh, snow-zombies don't seem to like it."

"If you say so," said Leo, running off.

Rip grabbed a shovel and swung it like a sword. "It's snombie-plowing time!" he said. "Heads are gonna roll!"

"Great plan," said Alexander. "Without heads, they'll crumble."

"How can I help, Salamander?" asked Nikki.

"You and I have another job to do," said Alexander. "*We* are going to put an end to those clinks!"

69

13 THE CLINKER

Alexander and Nikki followed the strange clinking sound up the snowy mountain.

"So what do you think is making that sound?" asked Nikki as they reached Lake Gloamy.

CLINK! CLINK! CLINK!

Alexander peered out across the icy lake. "I think we're about to find out," he said. "See that house, out in the middle of the lake?"

"Yeah," said Nikki. "Is it moving . . . ?"

Actually, it wasn't a house. It was a gigantic ice cube with icicle fangs, cold eyes, and blocky fists. It used its spiky knuckles to pull itself across the frozen lake.

"Oh, no!" shouted Alexander. "That ice block is headed this way!"

The monster skidded to a stop, spraying Alexander and Nikki with shaved ice.

"Hello, warm-bloods," it said. "Which one of you is the appetizer? And which is the main course?"

Alexander shivered. "You want to *eat* us?" he asked.

"I sure do!" said the monster. "I'm the ice-crusher! I'm made of ice, and I crush things. Kids, mostly. Right before I eat them. And right now, I'm ready to eat!"

"Uh, we don't taste very good," said Nikki, taking a step back.

"Oh, you're too warm to eat *now*," said the ice-crusher. "That's why I whipped up my snombies—to turn you campers into kid-pops. And then: chomp!"

The ice-crusher slammed its fists together.

Two more snombies rose up. They began windmilling their arms, hurling a flurry of snowballs at Alexander and Nikki.

"Run!" said Alexander.

Alexander turned and—**WHAM!**—crashed into the canoe rack. One of the canoes fell to the ground.

"Get in!" said Nikki. She grabbed a paddle. "We'll ride out of here!"

"Not so fast!" said the ice-crusher. The giant block of ice pressed its fists into the ground, lifting its body above Alexander and Nikki.

Nikki gave the canoe a shove as Alexander hopped in.

FWOOM! The monster's body came down like a sledgehammer, crushing the rest of the canoes. Alexander and Nikki's canoe shot down the mountain.

The monster raced after them.

"You can't out-sled me!" it yelled. "I'm *made* of ice!"

14 DON'T FLIP OUT

Watch out for that tree!" Alexander shouted.

"Gimme a break!" said Nikki. "I've never canoed on land before!"

They rocketed down the mountain, catching air on corners as Nikki tried to steer with her paddle.

FWOOSSSSSHHH! The ice-crusher sped closer. Alexander could feel its frosty breath on the back of his neck. "It's gaining on us!" he shouted.

SNAP! The monster chomped off the end of Nikki's oar, and spat out the splinters.

Nikki jammed her oar into the ground. The canoe banked to the right and tipped over, spilling Nikki and Alexander to the ground.

JAM!

KROMP!

The ice-crusher smacked into the canoe. The monster flipped end-over-end. It came down hard, wedging itself between two trees.

THUD!

"Awesome, Nikki! It's stuck!" said Alexander.

The ice-crusher roared. It pounded at the trees.

"Not for long!" said Nikki. "Let's move!"

They jumped back into the canoe and flew down the rest of the mountain.

They crash-landed into the huge salt pile near the campfire circle.

Alexander and Nikki tumbled out, dizzy but unhurt. They got to their feet.

The bonfire was much larger now. Rip stood nearby, warming his hands.

"Fire-safety Tip #9," said Rip. "Keep your bonfires small—except when snombies attack!"

"Nice work, Rip!" said Alexander. "But where are the other campers?"

"Did the snombies get them?" asked Nikki.

"No. They freaked out, so I sent them to the cabins," said Rip.

"What happened to the snombies?!" asked Alexander.

"Those weenies?" said Rip, smiling. "The first few fell to pieces after I knocked off their heads." He brushed snow from his sleeve. "That made the others mad, so they rushed at me. I just stayed by the fire while they melted into puddles."

"Great!" said Alexander, looking over his shoulder. "I'm hoping that we can melt the ice-crusher, too! It's the monster that's been making all the clinks."

"TIM-BERRRRRRR!" A voice echoed through the trees.

Up the mountain, two giant pine trees came crashing to the ground.

"Quick! Throw another log on the fire!" yelled Nikki. "We're about to have company."

15 ROYAL BLOCKHEAD

The ice-crusher barreled down the mountain.

Alexander, Rip, and Nikki waited in front of the fire pit.

"Ready?" whispered Alexander.

The monster pushed its fists into the ground like ski poles, picking up speed.

"I'm going to flatten you into baloney!" it roared.

"NOW!" Alexander cried.

The three friends dove to the side.

The ice-crusher slammed on the brakes, but it was too late. The monster skidded to a stop, right in the middle of the bonfire.

HISSSS!! A cloud of steam rose as flames flicked the monster's underside.

"Ha!" said Rip. "Fire-safety Rule #1: Never sit on a fire!"

But then: **CRUNNNK!!** The fire was gone. The flames had hardened into blue icicles.

"Do you think a little campfire can stop *me*?!" The monster laughed so hard, icicles fell from its eyes. Then it picked up the frozen bonfire and wore it like a crown. "Silly meat-creatures! I freeze out the summer sun! I *make* it snow! Fire can't hurt me!"

The ice-crusher pounded its fists together with a thunderous **CLINK!** The sound echoed through the mountains.

"ARISE, MY MINIONS, AND FREEZE THOSE ANNOYING KIDS!"

Hundreds of snombies shot up from the snow.

"To the canoe!" Alexander yelled. They ran loops all around the snombies, and dove behind the smashed-up canoe.

Heads spinning, the snowmen turned and twirled into one another like bumper cars.

"Make way, snow-for-brains!" hissed the ice-crusher. "The warm-bloods are hiding behind that canoe! I can hear them skittering around!"

The ice-crusher slid over to the splintered canoe, and plucked it from the salt pile.

Three white, roundish figures stood behind the canoe. They had no arms and no faces. One wore a floppy yellow hat.

The ice-crusher grinned, flashing a mouthful of jagged, icy teeth.

"Oh!" said the monster. "Nice work, snombies! You turned these pesky campers into kid-pops after all."

The ice-crusher cracked its knuckles. It pounded the white, roundish figures into flat lumps. And then it swallowed them.

16 SNOW MORE MR. ICE GUY

The ice-crusher smacked its icy lips. "Yuck!" it bellowed. "These kid-pops taste funny. They taste like"—its eyes widened—"SALT?!"

Alexander, Rip, and Nikki ran out from behind the salt mound.

"Gotchya, iceberg!" shouted Rip. "We made fake snow-kids out of good old ice-melting salt!"

"NOOOOOO!" howled the ice-crusher. The monster's face fell. And so did all of its other parts as it melted into a salty, slushy mess.

Then, as quick as a sneeze, three things happened:

1. The sun appeared in the sky.

2. The temperature shot up to ninety-nine degrees.

3. All the snow—and all the snombies—melted, turning the ground into a big mud pit.

Alexander, Rip, and Nikki danced in the mud.

Ranger Harry stepped into the clearing, dragging a load of wood. "Drat!" he said. "This weather is bananas!"

The ranger twisted the end of his beard. "Where'd the other campers go?"

"Back to the cabins," said Nikki.

"Okay, prairie dogs," said Ranger Harry. "It's been one weird morning. You should head back, too. I'll join you as soon as I put my sled away!"

"Yes, sir!" said Alexander.

The happy, tired, muddy, slushy friends walked toward the cabins.

Suddenly, Rip stopped. Something orange and pointy rested on a pile of leaves. "A snombie nose!" he said.

"Or just a carrot," said Nikki.

Rip grabbed the carrot, and—

FLOOP!

A large net swooped them up into a tree.

"I think we found Dottie's bunny trap!" said Nikki.

Alexander laughed. "Camp Rule #1: Nothing beats, uh, hanging around with your friends."

"Hanging around?" said Rip. "I don't get it." Nikki punched his arm.

Alexander fished in his backpack for the monster notebook. Then he added a new entry.

ICE-CRUSHER

A huge blockhead
who needs to
chill out.

HABITAT

Gloamy
Mountains.

DIET Frozen kid-pops.
(Hand-scooped by an army of snombies.)

CLINK! The ice-crusher creates snombies by clinking its fists together.

BEHAVIOR

This cold-hearted monster can make a blizzard on the hottest day.

WARNING! Fire cannot melt an ice-crusher! But 10,000 pinches of salt should do the trick!

TROY CUMMINGS

has no tail, no wings, no fangs, no claws, and only one head. As a kid, he believed that monsters might really exist. Today, he's sure of it.

BEHAVIOR This creature takes soccer lessons from his five-year-old.

HABITAT Troy Cummings lives in a nice little house that has nice little racoons on the roof.

 DIET Biscuits with honey.

EVIDENCE Few people believe that Troy Cummings is real. The only proof we have is that he supposedly wrote and illustrated The Eensy-Weensy Spider Freaks Out!, and Giddy-up, Daddy!

WARNING Keep your eyes peeled for more danger in The Notebook of Doom #8:

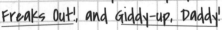

CHARGE OF THE LIGHTNING BUGS